Dear _____,

Disappear into this book.
Find magic everywhere you look.
Be wild, little one.

With love, _____

For Amalia,
who likes the bit about the fish
—D. E.

For my sons
—O. H.

Be Wild.

BLOOMSBURY CHILDREN'S BOOKS
Bloomsbury Publishing Inc., part of Bloomsbury Publishing Plc
1385 Broadway, New York, NY 10018

BLOOMSBURY, BLOOMSBURY CHILDREN'S BOOKS, and the Diana logo
are trademarks of Bloomsbury Publishing Plc

First published in Great Britain in May 2022 by Bloomsbury Publishing Plc
Published in the United States of America in April 2023
by Bloomsbury Children's Books

Text copyright © 2022 by Olivia Hope
Illustrations copyright © 2022 by Daniel Egnéus

Bloomsbury books may be purchased for business or promotional use. For information on bulk purchases please contact
Macmillan Corporate and Premium Sales Department at specialmarkets@macmillan.com

Library of Congress Cataloging-in-Publication Data
available upon request
ISBN 978-1-5476-1126-3 (hardcover) • ISBN 978-1-5476-1125-6 (e-book) • ISBN 978-1-5476-1127-0 (e-PDF)

Book design by Strawberrie Donnelly and Yelena Safronova
Typeset in 1786 GLC Fournier Narrow
Printed and bound in China by Leo Paper Products, Heshan, Guangdong
2 4 6 8 10 9 7 5 3 1

To find out more about our authors and books visit www.bloomsbury.com and sign up for our newsletters.

Little One

Olivia Hope

illustrated by
Daniel Egnéus

BLOOMSBURY
CHILDREN'S BOOKS

NEW YORK LONDON OXFORD NEW DELHI SYDNEY

Wake up early. Don't be shy.
This bright world can make you FLY!

Be **wild**, little one.

Make the world
your own playground.
Fill it with a noisy sound.

Stomp and stamp,
clap and cheer.

Be wild,
little one.

Sing your song for all to hear!

Cross
the
ocean,
sail
the
seas . . .

Trek in jungles,

climb up trees.

Swing along with
chimpanzees!

Be wild, little one.

Dive into the deepest blues . . .

Dig in sands for golden clues.
Grow a hero inside you.

Be wild, little one.

Chase tornadoes

high and low.

Storms will come,

but storms will go.

Run with wolves
through mountain snow.

Be **wild**, little one.

Dance with fireflies near and far.

Wish

on every shining star.

Magical—
that's
what
you
are.

Be wild, little one.

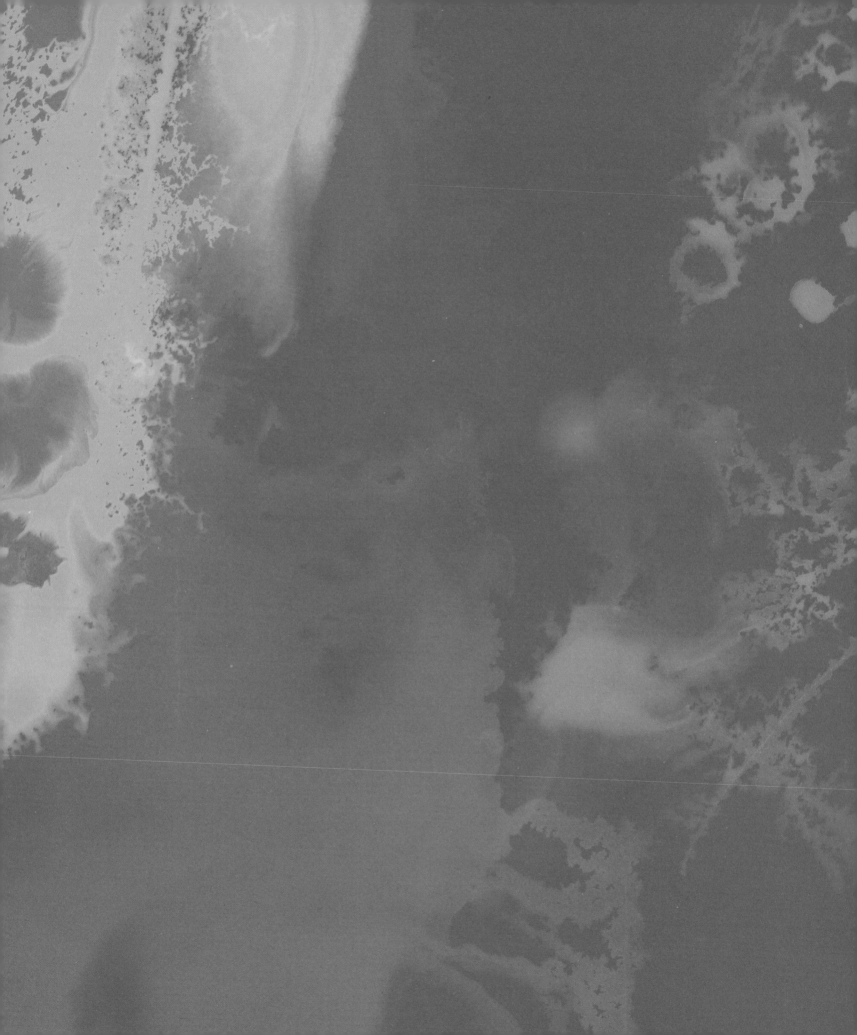